Night of Rebellion!

NICKOLAS FLUX and the Boston Tea Party

BY Nel Yomtov

ILLUSTRATED BY Dante Ginevra

CONSULTANT:

Richard Bell, PhD
Associate Professor of History
University of Maryland, College Park

CAPSTONE PRESS
a capstone imprint

Graphic Library is published by Capstone Press,
1710 Roe Crest Drive, North Mankato, Minnesota 56003
www.capstonepub.com

Library of Congress Cataloging-in-Publication Data
Yomtov, Nelson.
 Night of rebellion! : Nickolas Flux and the Boston Tea Party / by Nel
Yomtov ; illustrated by Dante Ginevra.
     pages cm.—(Graphic library. Nickolas Flux history chronicles)
  Summary: "In graphic novel format, follows the adventures of Nickolas
Flux as he travels back in time and must survive the Boston Tea Party"—
Provided by publisher.
  Includes bibliographical references and index.
  ISBN 978-1-4765-3946-1 (library binding)
  ISBN 978-1-4765-5150-0 (paperback)
  ISBN 978-1-4765-6007-6 (eBook PDF)
1. Boston Tea Party, Boston, Mass., 1773—Juvenile literature. 2. United
States—History—Colonial period, ca. 1600-1775—Juvenile literature.
3. Boston Tea Party, Boston, Mass., 1773—Comic books, strips, etc.
4. United States—History—Colonial period, ca. 1600-1775—Comic
books, strips, etc. I. Ginevra, Dante, 1976- illustrator. II. Title.
  E215.7.Y66 2014
  973.3'115—dc23   2013028001

Photo Credits:
Design Elements: Shutterstock (backgrounds)

Editor's note:
A direct quotation, noted in   type, appears on the following page:
Page 13, from *Samuel Adams* by James K. Hosmer (New York:
Houghton Mifflin Company, 1898).

EDITOR
Christopher L. Harbo

DESIGNER
Ashlee Suker

ART DIRECTOR
Nathan Gassman

PRODUCTION SPECIALIST
Kathy McColley

Printed in the United States of America in Stevens Point, Wisconsin.
092013   007767WZS14

TABLE OF
CONTENTS

LENDALL
PITTS

FRANCIS ROTCH

TEA PARTY
REBELS

Rotch will be here any moment with Governor Hutchinson's decision.

Who's Rotch?

Francis Rotch. He's the owner of the *Dartmouth*. It is one of three British tea ships in the harbor waiting to be unloaded.

He's here. Let's hear him out ...

Governor Hutchinson won't allow me to sail my ship out of the harbor.

I will have to unload the tea by tomorrow, although it is against my will.

FLUX FACT

About 5,000 people attended the meeting at the Old South Meeting House. Some historians believe Adams' quotation above was a signal to dump the tea.

CHAPTER THREE
AN ACT OF TREASON

FLUX FACT

Lendall Pitts was an active member of the Sons of Liberty. American patriots formed this group to protect the colonists' rights and to protest the taxes by the British government.

FLUX FACT

Many historians doubt that the protestors wore full Mohawk Indian dress. Firsthand reports say that most of the participants disguised themselves with ragged blankets and soot-smeared faces. Some wore feathers in their hair.

FLUX FACT

The Boston Tea Party lasted three hours. In all, 342 chests containing 90,000 pounds (41 metric tons) of tea were thrown overboard. In today's money, the cost of the tea would be equal to about $1 million.

CHAPTER FOUR
DISASTER!

Stop! Stop! I meant no harm.

We're here to destroy tea—not line our pockets with it.

I beg you ... please ... stop!

WHACK!

THUMP!

FLUX FACT

Captain Charles O'Connor owned an inn and a stable in Boston. His attempt to steal tea endangered the secrecy of the Tea Party. It made him very unpopular in Boston.

A MEMENTO FROM THE PAST

The present

Whoa! That was close.

The Boston Tea Party may have given colonists hope to fight Britain for political representation ...

... but it almost cost me my life.

Did you find the tea, Nick?

FLUX FILES

FRENCH AND INDIAN WAR

The war fought between the British and the French in America is called the French and Indian War (1754-1763). American Indian groups fought for both sides in the conflict. Britain won the war and established itself as the main colonial power in the eastern part of North America.

TEA POPULARITY

Tea was as important to the colonists as coffee is to adults today. Everyone drank it—rich and poor, young and old. It was easy to make and transport. By the 1760s, the total population of the colonies was only about 1.6 million people. But Americans were using 1.2 million tons (1 million metric tons) of tea each year!

BRITISH INACTION

British authorities in Boston did nothing to stop the Tea Party. Admiral John Montagu, commander of the British Navy, saw what was happening from his house near Griffin's Wharf. Officers and sailors aboard the British gunship in Boston Harbor also watched the destruction of the tea. The British claimed that they could not break up the protestors without shooting into the crowd and thereby injuring innocent bystanders.

MORE TEA PARTIES

Other tea parties took place in New York, New Jersey, and Maryland shortly after the one in Boston. A second tea party occurred in Boston on March 7, 1774.

INTOLERABLE ACTS

When news of the Tea Party reached Great Britain, Parliament quickly passed a set of laws. The colonists called these laws the Intolerable Acts. Boston Harbor was closed to all incoming and outgoing ships until the destroyed tea was paid for. Special town meetings were outlawed. Colonists could no longer secretly plan actions against British authorities. Another act allowed British officers to house their soldiers in American homes throughout the colonies.

GLOSSARY

BYSTANDER (BYE-stan-dur)—someone who is at a place where something happens to someone else

CARGO (KAHR-goh)—the goods carried by a ship, vehicle, or aircraft

COLONIST (KAH-luh-nist)—a person who settles in a new territory that is governed by his or her home country

COLONY (KAH-luh-nee)—a place that is settled by people from another country and is controlled by that country

CUSTOMS AGENT (KUHS-tuhms AY-juhnt)—a government official who collects taxes and gives permission for ships to enter or leave a country

DUTY (DOO-tee)—a tax or charge on goods brought into a country

EXPORT (EK-sport)—to send and sell goods to other countries

IMPORT (IM-port)—to bring goods into one country from another

INTOLERABLE (in-TOL-ur-uh-buhl)—difficult to endure

PARLIAMENT (PAHR-luh-muhnt)—the group of British people who have been elected to make the laws in Great Britain

PATRIOT (PAY-tree-uht)—a person who loves and fights for his or her country

PROTEST (pro-TEST)—to object to something strongly and publicly

REPRESENTATION (rep-ri-zen-TAY-shuhn)—the right of being represented by someone, especially in the legislature of a government

TAX (TAKS)—money collected from a country's citizens to help pay for running the government

TYRANNY (TIHR-uh-nee)—a cruel or unfair government in which all power is in the hands of a single ruler

READ MORE

CUNNINGHAM, KEVIN. *The Boston Tea Party.* Cornerstones of Freedom. Danbury, Conn.: Children's Press, 2013.

GONDOSCH, LINDA. *How Did Tea and Taxes Spark a Revolution? and Other Questions About the Boston Tea Party.* Six Questions of American History. Minneapolis: Lerner Publications, 2011.

PERRITANO, JOHN. *The Causes of the American Revolution.* Understanding the American Revolution. New York: Crabtree Publishing Company, 2013.

INTERNET SITES

FactHound offers a safe, fun way to find Internet sites related to this book. All sites on FactHound have been researched by our staff.

Here's all you do:

Visit *www.facthound.com*

Type in this code: 9781476539461

Super-cool stuff!

Check out projects, games and lots more at
www.capstonekids.com

INDEX

ABOUT THE AUTHOR

Nel Yomtov is a writer of children's nonfiction books and graphic novels. He specializes in writing about history, country studies, science, and biography. His graphic novel adaptation, Jason and the Golden Fleece, published by Stone Arch Books was a winner of the 2009 Moonbeam Children's Book Award and the 2011 Lighthouse Literature Award. Nel is an avid American military history buff and has written two additional graphic novels for Capstone, True Stories of World War I and True Stories of the Civil War. He lives in the New York City area.